This one's for Drinda,
who has a wide heart
—A.T.

To my mother, Mary Hartwell Mavor,
for sharing an artful life.
—S.M.

In the Heart
Text copyright © 2001 by Ann Turner
Illustrations copyright © 2001 by Salley Mavor
Printed in the U.S.A. All rights reserved. www.harperchildrens.com

Library of Congress Cataloging-in-Publication Data   Turner, Ann Warren.
In the heart / by Ann Turner; artwork by Salley Mavor.
p.   cm.
Summary: A girl describes the important parts of her day, from the warmth of
the morning sun to the moon overhead at night.
ISBN 0-06-023730-9. — ISBN 0-06-023731-7 (lib. bdg.)
[1. Day—Fiction.] I. Mavor, Salley, ill.   II. Title.
PZ7.T8535ln   2001 • 98-36604 • [E]—dc21 • CIP • AC

Typography by Hui Hui Su-Kennedy
1 2 3 4 5 6 7 8 9 10
❖
First Edition

HARTS

Heart

The heart of the day
is the sun:
a warm blanket on my eyes
and nose and feet,
a gold hat for my head.

The heart of the house
is my kitchen:
orange cat by my seat,
a muffin warms my hand,
talk like clouds of steam.

February

1	2	3	4	5	6	7
8	9	10	11	12	13	14
15	16	17	18	19	20	21
22	23	24	25	26	27	28

The heart of the yard
is my tree:
a branch where I am queen,
a swing to touch the bark,
and ground to hold my feet.

The heart of the street
is my sidewalk:
one jump, two jump hopscotch,
I dance over rope,
my ball rolls away.

The heart of the town
is my school:
valentines in windows,
I color mine red,
a heart for everyone.

The heart of bedtime
is my story:
your knees my chair,
your words in my hair,
pictures for dreams.

The heart of the night
is the moon.
It hides behind trees,
rides on a cloud,
touches Mama's muffin bowl,
hangs on the tip of my tree,

slides down the dark street,
shines on the school windows,
rests on the hand of my sleeping friend,

and comes back to me—
deep in the pillow,
deep in the bed,
deep in the heart of
the house.

and smell the sunshine.

I pull up the covers,

When I say goodnight,
	and worry about shadows in my room,

With arms full of dancing partners,
we waltz into the house to sort
and fold and stack.

After a while of this and that,
we empty the clothesline and do-si-do
with sheets that flip and flap.

and in the afternoon,
the maybe of rain.

filling everything on the clothesline
with smells, stories, and wind,

and the sunshine finishes its job,

Mommy and me finish our job,

and falling up, then caught.

I like to get caught!

lost, then found, and lost again—

We play and hide
in the wet folds of laundry.

The breeze catches
        our sheet and floats the fabric.

Mommy and me.

and the clothespins,

the neighborhood dogs
barking out their stories,

for the laughing birds,
   the insects floating by,

sweet and spicy,

for the warm air,

I get my laundry ready

On washing day,

Published in the United States of America by Star Bright Books, Inc.

The name Star Bright Books and the Star Bright Books logo are registered
trademarks of Star Bright Books, Inc. Please visit: www.starbrightbooks.com.
For bulk orders, email: orders@starbrightbooks.com, or call customer service at: (617) 354-1300.

Hardback ISBN-13: 978-1-59572-635-3
Star Bright Books / MA / 00107130
Printed in China (C&C) 10 9 8 7 6 5 4 3 2 1

Paperback ISBN-13: 978-1-59572-636-0
Star Bright Books / MA / 00107130
Printed in China (C&C) 10 9 8 7 6 5 4 3 2 1

Library of Congress Cataloging-in-Publication Data

Anderson, Constance.
 Smelling sunshine / written and illustrated by Constance Anderson.
    p. cm.
 Summary: Celebrates the special moments the ordinary task of doing laundry brings
when shared by a parent and child.
 ISBN 978-1-59572-635-3 (hardcover book) -- ISBN 978-1-59572-636-0 (pbk. book)
[1. Laundry--Fiction. 2. Parent and child--Fiction.] I. Title.
 PZ7.A525Sme 2013
 [E]--dc23
                                      2012031053

Smelling Sunshine

by

Constance Anderson

STAR BRIGHT BOOKS
Cambridge, Massachusetts